A SHORT STORY OF LOVE AND **REVENGE.**

DEBRA ROSE

Writing Roses

Contents

The Office

*C*lack, clack, clack.

My fingers flew across the keyboard, the rhythm echoing in the small office and fending off my worried, intrusive thoughts. For over an hour, the white screen and steady stream of words had fully captured my attention. Even the buzz of my phone notifications hadn't broken through my hyper-focused haze.

And then, mid-sentence, it stopped. The flow that had captured me ran dry as I stumbled over an inconsistency in my gathered facts, and I swallowed the groan that wanted to escape.

The CEO of Wine and Croft had embezzled millions of dollars and fled the country, but did he land in Panama or Costa Rica? It would make a difference when it came time to extradite... that was, if he was ever found.

Before I could even start pulling up my main research documents, my phone buzzed again. I reached for it, licking my lips as I did so and tasted the stale dryness of my own mouth after going too long without a beverage. Subconsciously, I reached for my water bottle with one hand as my thumb pulled up my text messages.

You still coming tonight?

Woman! Where are you? Place is jumping!

Sofia Holly, if you're still at the office, I'm going to skin you!

My eyes widened as they shot to the clock, seeing it was nearly 7pm. The groan finally escaped. I quickly saved the article and shut down the PC, then realized my water bottle was completely empty. Smacking my lips, I tried to work some moisture back into my mouth as I gathered my purse and folded my jacket over my arm. I shot a quick message to Clara before heading to the door.

I'm otw!

I pulled my office door shut behind me and turned toward the elevator but was stopped by the low rumble of a man clearing his throat. My blood turned to ice in my veins as I turned toward Robert, my senior editor. Crystal blue eyes stared at me over the rim of his glasses as he stood outside his office door.

I had thought I'd escaped by staying late. Apparently, I was wrong.

"I assume you were finishing up the Backlight article for me?" His voice grated on every nerve in my body. It was always a command. Always an half-hidden insult, even when he was on his 'better' behavior. The way he wore his salt-and-pepper gray hair slicked back from his thin face embodied his whole personality.

"I just have some finishing touches left. I'll have it over to you first thing in the morning." I focused on the fact that I was walking out the door for the night and pulled from deep down to add a jovial tone to my voice. The smile that followed almost felt natural. Almost.

Rob exhaled loudly through his nose as he made a show of folding his arms across his chest. He needed me to know he didn't approve.

However, if he thought I found him intimidating, he was wrong. He was simply annoying.

"Deadline is noon. Do I need to tidy up the article for you, Sofia?"

Claws of ice ran down my spine, and the smile froze on my face. His snide remark was nothing more than an intended slight because we both knew I never missed a deadline. Likewise, Rob never missed an opportunity to remind his underlings of his position, despite the fact he wasn't the one with the talent.

"I've got it covered." My words came short and clipped, and I let the jovial mask shatter.

"Make sure you do." He didn't miss a beat, and by the smug smile that crossed his face, he believed he had gotten one up on me. It was all I could do to not shake my head as I turned away.

The words he sent chasing me down the hall spun me back in his direction. "Red looks good on you."

My jaw dropped in shock. The change in his tone was palpable, and he had one eyebrow raised as he smirked at me. I didn't bother replying as I turned away again, wanting to escape.

As I stomped down the hall, his voice carried after me. "Have a good evening."

I left the building, fuming with anger, but I realized he *had* won. When he couldn't get the better of me with work related topics, he had shifted gears and caught me off guard.

"What a prick," I muttered as I jerked open my car door and slid in.

Once safe inside, locked away from any torment Robert Wise might throw at me, I let my head fall back against the seat and took a deep breath. My eyes stayed closed until the buzz of my phone opened them again. I looked down to see I had missed another three messages from Clara.

Get your ass over here!

I got our normal booth.

Your wings are getting cold!

Grinning, I let all my work troubles fade away and sent back one message.

Is he there??

Clara would know who I was talking about. I didn't need to name him since he was the only thing I could think about if I wasn't actively distracted.

Nikolaj Dunkan.

Nikolaj had started working at the Morning Press around six months ago, although I rarely bumped into him since he worked in the printing department. It wasn't until he started joining us at the Oasis that I really noticed him. To be specific, it was his dark eyes that I noticed first and how they seemed to see everything, catch everything, drink everything in.

Even me.

The memory of when I first saw him looking at me was enough to make me shiver. His eyes had lingered on my lips before rising to my eyes, and it was only then that he formally introduced himself. Despite that first glance, he was more down to earth than I expected; easy to talk to and willing to listen to all my crazy stories.

I never could get the nerve to ask him out, and then two weeks ago, he had vanished. I found out from his department head that Nik had taken sick leave, but that didn't help the fact he wasn't answering calls or text messages... from anyone. Something about it just didn't feel right.

I pulled into a parking spot at the Oasis and grabbed my phone to see one last message from Clara.

Your boy's not here.

I stared at the bright neon sign of our local bar and softly muttered, "Nik... where are you?"

The Oasis

As soon as I stepped across the threshold and entered the bar proper, the thump of the loud music drove all thoughts of work away. With the familiar noise in my head, I pushed through the small crowd and bee-lined to the booths that lined the back wall. Clara was there as promised with a handful of our other bar-fly buddies, and I sank down next to her, wasting no time as I pulled my plate of chicken wings in front of me.

I was starving.

"I knew it!" Clara reached over and pinched the fabric of my shirt between her fingers. "You haven't even gone home to change."

"What?" I spoke around a bite of wing and rubbed the stray buffalo sauce off my lip with a finger. "This shirt looks good on me."

Clara smacked her lips so loud I heard the pop over the drone of the music.

Leaning over to whisper, I said, "I know it looks good because Rob said so."

"He didn't!" she gasped as her eyes widened. Then, after a nod from me, she tsked and added, "What a pig."

Another wing went into my mouth as my comment spread around the table. Vince, who sat across from me, leaned forward and said, "Honey, own it. Yes, you look great in that shirt and don't let that man get to you. You wear what *you* want to, how you want."

"I bet she wore it for Nik," Jane added with a sly grin.

A blush instantly heated my cheeks, but the worry followed right after. This was the first time I had seen Jane in a while, and since she didn't work at the press, I guessed no one had filled her in. Suddenly, the food turned sour in my mouth, and I let the wing drop to the plate below.

"Oh." Jane's face fell. "Is he still sick? Is it serious?"

As I wiped my fingers off on my napkin, Clara filled her in. "We don't know. Complete radio silence."

"My god," Jane gasped. "Has anyone been to his apartment to make sure he's not…"

Thankfully, her words cut off short as my eyes shot to her. I said, "If what his department head says is true, they did."

"Empty," Clara added.

A tray plopped down on the table, carrying a large pitcher of beer and five glasses. Joe, who was already passing the glasses around, said, "Let your cups overflow. They shall be empty no more!"

Vince grabbed Joe's arm and pulled him down to sit in the booth next to him. "You're such a nerd."

Joe leaned over long enough to nuzzle against Vince's cheek before grabbing the pitcher to pour. "And that's why you love me."

"It's true."

"So what are we really talking about? What's empty?" Joe asked.

"Nik's apartment," Jane answered. "I didn't know he was still missing!"

"Oo, we're talking about Nik?" Joe perked up as he asked. "Do y'all wanna know what I think?"

I grabbed a glass and brought it to my lips as I turned my gaze to the rest of the bar. As much as the man was on my mind, I wasn't ready to share my thoughts. Everyone already knew I had been crushing on him.

"*I* think he's an undercover FBI agent, searching for that serial killer out there." Joe made a show of shivering before leaning into Vince. "Someone that sexy has to have a few secrets to uncover."

"Maybe a little trauma to unpack," Vince added.

Joe straightened. "Now, why would you say that?"

"Oh, don't tell me you didn't see it too." Vince waved a hand in the air as he spoke. "Those wounded puppy dog eyes. Always silent and brooding."

"He wasn't brooding." The words came out of my mouth before I could stop them. All eyes turned to me, and I shifted uncomfortably. "He was just... very observant."

"He sure liked to observe you, that's for sure," Joe muttered right before gulping down a swig of beer.

Clara gasped beside me as a thought dawned on her. "What if he *is* the killer?"

"Clara!" Jane's eyes were wide with shock.

"Well." Clara shrugged. "Have they found any new bodies these past two weeks?"

I half chuckled, half groaned. "There were plenty before he moved here. He's not the killer."

"So, hot undercover detective, then," Joe added proudly as he squirmed in his seat.

"Alright." I slapped my hands on the table, interrupting whatever Vince was about to say. "No more talk about Nik, serial killers, or chauvinistic, asshole bosses."

"Wait, what did Rob do this time?" Joe glanced up, confused.

Vince patted Joe's hand. "I'll tell you later, Honey."

Propping an elbow on the table, I took the time to point at everyone until all eyes were on me and said, "Tonight, I declare this a drama and gossip-free zone. I'm leaving all the bullshit for tomorrow."

"Cheers to that!" Vince was the first to raise his glass, and everyone followed suit.

I downed my beer and reached for the pitcher to pour another. I *would not* spend another night worrying about Nik Dunkan.

Memories

“I’m fine! I’m fine,” I giggled as I stumbled off the curb and careened into Joe. He was a sturdy man and easily caught me, wrapping his arm around my shoulders to steady me.

“I think you may have hit it a little hard tonight.”

I sighed and let my head fall back on his shoulder, looking up at the stars. The cool night air felt so good. “Working for Rob Wise can do that to a person.”

“We aren’t judging,” Joe answered quickly. “Honestly, I don’t know how you do it.”

“Honey, let’s make good life decisions tonight.” Vince was standing in front of me with his hand out, and I reluctantly handed over the keys. It wasn’t like it was going to put either one of them out since they lived one floor below me. I just hated taking advantage of it.

“Come on, love.” Joe pulled me along, opening the passenger side door as Vince climbed in the drivers side. “I’m going to stop by the corner store and grab you some Gatorade. We don’t need you hungover when you face that horrible tyrant tomorrow.”

I giggled again and planted a finger in Joe's chest. "I finished the Backlight article last week. I've been working on the Jones' Heirs and didn't tell him."

"Good for you!" Joe beamed a smile, then pushed me toward the open car door. "I don't know what any of that means, but it sounds fantastic."

I half-sat, half-fell into the seat. Joe leaned over to buckle me in, and I slapped his hands away. "I am *not* that drunk."

Joe backed away, his hands up and fingers spread wide. "Okay, okay. See you at home, love."

I turned my head to look at Vince. "Hi."

He stifled a laugh, then rose an eyebrow as he pointedly looked at the seat belt I had yet to buckle. My fingers felt numb and clumsy as I grasped it in my hands, but snapped the clasp into place on my second try. I flashed a triumphant smirk, which earned me a pat on the hand. Then we were off.

The car was filled with my off-key singing the whole ride home, but Vince was singing along with me. I didn't even realize we were home until the car stopped. Before he was able to drag me out of the car, Joe was already pulling up in their blue sedan.

"I thought he was stopping by the store," I mumbled as Joe came to join us.

Vince chuckled as we headed to our building. "I drove slow."

I stopped at their apartment door and turned to Joe, hand outstretched for the purple bottle of Gatorade he held. "How much do I owe you?"

"A beer, and you get to drive next time."

"Got it," I said, already twisting the top off the bottle. My throat was so dry it felt like I hadn't drank anything all day. "Same time tomorrow?"

"You sure your okay making it up those stairs in those heels?" Vince asked as he handed back my keys.

I glanced down at the black heels I wore. Even though they were open-toed with an ankle strap, the short three-inch stiletto heel was modest enough for work. "Good point."

Leaning against the wall, I reached down to first loosen the clasp on one shoe, then the other, then lifted both shoes high as I took a bow. Vince actually clapped.

"Tomorrow!" I said, pointing a finger at them as I stumbled to the stairs. Once my hand was on the railing, I felt steady enough to work my way up. One step at a time, and I found the rough grate of the stairs on my bare feet was actually sobering. The men didn't enter their apartment, dutifully watching me until I was turning the key in my door.

My dark, lonely apartment greeted me, and the joy of the night began to dissipate. With a sigh, I dropped my heels by the door and took another deep swig of the Gatorade. The strong drunken buzz was fading, and I had a decision to make. Do the responsible thing; take a shower and head to bed, or fetch another cold beer that was waiting on me in the fridge.

I glanced toward the bathroom of my one bedroom apartment and knew what waited for me there. I was going to fume over Rob's chauvinism and worry over Nik's disappearance.

And just that easy, my mind started to spiral. Was he the killer? A victim? The sexy undercover detective? I rolled my eyes, unable to match Nik's down-to-earth personality with any of those scenarios. My thumbnail scratched at the plastic on the bottle as I stood in the dark entryway and considered who Nik really was. What did I know about him?

Nik Dunkan had worked in the print department at our Morning Press for less than six months. He didn't love his job, but he could do it well. I knew this because I vividly remembered the way his dark eyes fixed on mine as he told me. I could still hear his rich, baritone voice detailing his work routine, and I had continued to ask him questions just to keep him talking. There was a desperate need inside me that could only be fed by that smooth baritone rumble.

But we only ever really talked about work. He didn't *seem* like the type that would drop everything and run, so my wayward theories always landed on foul play. I found no comfort in that scenario either.

My decision made, I padded over to the fridge to exchange the Gatorade for the beer. As I passed the dining room mirror and caught a glimpse of myself in the blood-red, silk shirt, I groaned loudly and stomped my foot in agitation. Rob's creepy words rolled over again in my mind, and I suddenly couldn't get the thing off fast enough. I threw it on the table in disgust and mourned the loss of what had been my new favorite article of clothing.

Popping the top off my beer, I cast a look back at myself in the mirror. Wearing nothing but my black pencil skirt and plain chemise, I lifted a brow as I studied my reflection. I pulled the clips from my hair and shook out the dark strands to bounce around my shoulders. Striking a seductive pose, I winked at myself and giggled. If only Nik had seen me like this.

The smile faded, and I turned to the balcony to stare out at the city.

"Where are you, Nik?" I whispered to the glass.

I had nothing else to do, so I remained standing there for many moments, occasionally sipping on my beer. My mind dwelled on that last night I had spent with Nik before he disappeared, reliving every moment.

We had been at the Oasis, of course, and I had lingered longer than usual just so I could spend more time with him. As the others trickled out to head home, Nik and I found ourselves alone in our booth. We had talked for what seemed like hours in an easy and comfortable conversation.

At one point, talk of Rob had bubbled to the surface. It hadn't been my ideal topic of conversation, but it was too easy to vent my frustrations. I wasn't all that surprised to hear Nik confess he had butted-heads with Rob a few times. When I told Nik about his sexist behavior, he was appalled. Even though I was skeptical at how sincere Nik was, throughout the course of our conversation, I began to believe him.

Before we parted ways that night, Nik walked me to my car and said, "I've got a friend who works in HR. I'll reach out to see if there's anything we can do about Rob."

"You don't have to do that," I had protested. "Really. I was only venting."

He smiled then, sweet and innocent, and any thought of telling him 'no' fled. I hadn't been looking for a white knight to save me, but I had to admit that I was sucked into the fantasy of Nik being my hero.

He sealed that fantasy when he leaned over and kissed my forehead. "Good night, Sofia," he had whispered, the tone of his voice more of a promise than his words. "I'll see you tomorrow."

And that was the last time I saw him.

Grumbling at myself for getting lost in memories, I grabbed a blanket to wrap around my shoulders and slid open the balcony door. I padded out onto the cold, hard concrete and took a deep breath of the crisp air. The sounds of the night enveloped me, and I lost myself in the darkness.

"Hello, Sofia."

Come In

The smooth voice shattered my serenity, replacing it with fear and panic. My name was whispered, caressed as it was slowly spoken, and I screamed before the voice went silent. Jumping back against the railing, the beer bottle slipped from my hand to shatter into a foamy mess of glass and suds.

"Don't move," The dark figure spoke, and I could see him patting his hands in the air. Was he trying to calm me? My mind was racing, but my body was frozen in fright. I had the blanket wrapped tight around me, not that it would shield me from anything.

"Don't move," the voice spoke again, and a flicker of recognition went off in my head. "You don't want you to cut yourself."

My heart was currently doing a beautiful rendition of a five-piece drum solo, and my head swam from the sudden head rush. But yes, I recognized him. That warm voice that had previously been my source of comfort was now what scared the shit out of me.

"Nik?" The softest whisper escaped. I still had difficulty breathing, but the shadow on my balcony heard. He shifted until the dim light from my apartment lit up his face, and I gasped. "Nik!"

The excitement bubbled up, mixing with the adrenaline and alcohol, and the over-joyed part of my brain squished any logic and sense that tried to rise to the surface. I took a single step forward, forgetting what happened less than a minute ago, and cried out as a shard of glass sliced into the bottom of my foot.

"Damnit!" I muttered as I clenched my jaw and fell back against the railing. I lifted my foot, propping it against my knee, and spotted the dark shard from the beer bottle. It stuck out from the arch of my foot, and a small drop of blood had seeped along the edge.

I glanced up at Nik, seeing that he had retreated to the shadows again, and for the first time, a critical thought climbed its way through the drunken haze and filled me with caution.

"How... How long have you been up here?" I glanced at the fire escape, then back at the shadows, suddenly wary. "Any why not use the front door?"

"I didn't want to cause you problems if I was seen here," he said simply. Easily. "I know Vince and Joe like to talk."

Of course, I thought, buying his explanation. *He doesn't want to start any rumors. How sweet!*

"Are you hurt?" The concern radiating in his voice triggered something inside me, causing a warm, restless tingle to swell through my body.

Blushing, I looked down to inspect the wound. It didn't seem so bad as the shard was barely hanging onto the surface of the skin. Wincing against the perceived pain, I plucked the glass free. It came away much easier than I expected, although a thick stream of blood followed.

"I guess it was deeper than I thought," I mumbled as a small drop of blood splattered on the concrete. Still, it wasn't terrible, but as I flicked the shard of glass away, I glanced at the carpet, knowing my landlord would kill me if I got bloodstains on it. Without fully thinking it through, I shrugged the blanket off my shoulders and wrapped it around my foot.

There. That should do it.

After all, a blanket was much easier to replace than carpet.

"I just need a minute," I said as I hobbled inside, making damn sure I was stepping on the blanket and not the carpet. Even after I made it to the kitchen tile, I didn't spill another drop of blood. "It'll just take a second to bandage this up. You don't need to stand there shivering in the cold."

But there was no answer, or at least not one I heard while fishing for a bandage. By the time I found one, the wound had stopped bleeding, and I realized there had not been any movement from the balcony.

"Nik?" I called out softly.

Nothing.

Unable to move until I finished dressing my foot, I quickly cleaned and dried it off before pressing on the bandage. All the while, my eyes were darting to the open balcony door. It remained dark and empty.

In the silence, doubt weaved through the excitement, and I became fully aware that I didn't know Nik as well as I wanted to. It had been my own dreams and fantasies that had filled in the pieces of a puzzle I desperately wanted to put together. The doubt was steadily morphing into fear, and only one thought rose in my mind.

Why was he here now?

"Nik?" I questioned the air again, taking slow steps toward the balcony. The gentle night wind played with the curtains, and they lazily billowed back and forth. It caused shadows to dance along the walls, and I tried to ignore what was exciting and romantic a few moments ago was quickly turning eerie.

I stopped in the middle of my living room as my courage and curiosity failed me. Unable to force myself to take another step, the light breeze that swept in caused my arms to pebble with gooseflesh. I wrapped my arms around myself, suddenly missing my blanket. For the briefest of seconds, I wondered if I had gotten lost in a drunken dream. *Had* Nik really been there?

My eyes dropped to the dark sparkling glass that used to be my beer bottle. My mind wandered, and I thought of cleaning it up, but I also thought of just leaving it for the morning. I could simply close the door on my vivid dream and sleep off the rest of the alcohol.

"I'm sorry." The voice came from the darkness of the night, beyond my little apartment living room. I sucked in a breath, holding it as I waited for more. Then, the shadows shifted, and the large frame of Nik Dunkan filled my balcony door. "I never meant to startle you."

I released the breath in a relieved sigh, thankful I hadn't imagined it. Him. The light from my kitchen lit his face, which was even more beautiful than I remembered. All the doubt and fear that had been welling up suddenly drained away to nothing.

Nik was alive. Nik was here. Nik was real.

His eyes glittered, dark and smoldering, and I swallowed. He saw me, every part of me, and I watched as his gaze lowered to my legs and slowly rose to my hips, my waist, my breasts, until they locked on to mine. The thin camisole and skirt I wore wasn't enough to shield me. I was stripped bare, and I knew in that instant I wanted more. Needed more.

Licking my lips and remembering how to breathe, I whispered, "Please, come in."

Keep Reading

S everal seconds passed in silence as our eyes remained locked. Finally, Nik took a single, hesitant step into my apartment.

"I don't want to keep you. I just wanted to drop something off," Nik said, and his eyes dropped to my foot. "Are you okay?"

I glanced down at my bare feet and wiggled my toes. The pain from the cut was already faded, and I'd forgotten about it until Nik's reminder. The only thing I could think about was Nik. How close he was. How good he looked. How good he smelled.

"I'm fine," I said, unable to think of anything else. I wasn't in the mood to talk anyway. Instead, my eyes drank in everything about his appearance. He wore brown cowboy boots, a dark pair of jeans, and a tight, black V-neck that was probably at least two sizes too small. It clung to every overly defined muscle on his chest, and I bit my lip, nearly overwhelmed by the urge to rip it off him.

Nik didn't seem to notice as he nodded and pulled what looked like a tube from his back pocket. It took me a moment to realize it was a bundle of rolled-up paper. "I did some research on Rob, but the more I found, the worse it got."

I frowned. I wasn't expecting talk of Rob Wise. Just the mention of his name immediately brought me back to my senses. "What do you mean?"

Nik glanced down at the bundle in his hands, his thumb fidgeting with the edges of the paper. Then he held it out for me, and I took a couple steps closer to him to grab it, putting me right next to him. It was hard to ignore how close our bodies were, but the curiosity over what was written on those pages drew my attention.

"What is this?" I asked, pulling the papers open. There were more sheets bundled together than I had initially realized.

"Just... I think it's better if you see for yourself."

I glanced up at him, wondering why he had turned so cryptic. "This is what you've been doing for the past two weeks?"

"Well," he started. "Not the whole time. I found a... friend that helped me get the information."

Again, I frowned but dropped my eyes to the bundle in my hands and gravitated toward the light in the kitchen. I read the name on the first page out loud. "Rebecca Tyler. I remember her. When I started at the press, she was a journalist but wasn't there for very long."

Nik stood silent behind me as I read. My eyes darted to the header on the page. I had overlooked it due to the print being so small, but there it was.

Morning Press Inappropriate Conduct Report Form.

I gasped as my eyes scanned the rest of the page. "This is against Rob!"

"Keep reading."

I did as instructed. "Company party. Rob Wise allegedly made unwanted contact with Rebecca Tyler in the kitchenette of the Morning Press."

My eyes shot to Nik, searching for an explanation. Nik cleared his throat and said, "Rebecca quit less than a week later. They buried the report after that."

"How—"

"Keep reading," he said again. He rolled his shoulders, distracting me for a moment. Then, he took a step back toward the still open balcony door and lazily leaned against the frame.

That wasn't the only thing that was loose about his appearance. Usually, he had always been clean-cut, almost stiff at times, but his new relaxed posture went along with his tousled hair. At work, every strand had always been in perfect place, but this... this begged me to run my fingers through it.

My lips parted as I took a deep breath, and my fingers crumpled the paper in my hands. It was enough to remind me I needed to drag my eyes away before I got caught staring. The man already had one foot out the door, literally.

Once again, the words on the paper drew my focus, and I flipped to the second page. "Jessica Atwell reported being detained in the parking garage and assaulted by an unknown assailant." I read from another Morning Press header, although this was a different form for Sexual Assault. "Atwell. I know that name."

"She was there two years before you started, but she was an editor," Nik filled in. "She was eventually fired."

My mouth was suddenly dry. I flipped through the following three sheets: more reports from Jessica, two Inappropriate Conduct, and one Sexual Harassment.

"Were these buried too?" I held them up as I glanced at Nik.

"Yes." The single-word answer was chilling, and I felt my stomach drop. I looked down at the reports, catching mention of unwanted massages and other physical contact, when Nik whispered, "Keep reading."

I paused, unsure if I wanted to keep going down this path, but after a moment, I flipped to the next page. This time the header wasn't from the Morning Press. Instead, it was a police report from a town in Arkansas. It was a report on a missing woman dated over ten years ago. I stumbled to the table and sank into the chair as I saw the woman's name.

Dorothy Wise.

"What is this?" I croaked, unable to steady my voice.

Nik finally moved from the doorway and came to stand at my side. Somehow, the darkness spreading from the reports didn't seem as frightening with Nik standing so close.

"That was his first wife," he said, and there was a coldness in Nik's voice that made me shiver. I glanced up at him, seeing the anger on his face, and I understood he was outraged. Then he said two words that I was dreading to hear. "Keep reading."

I looked back at the report lying in front of me and anxiously rubbed my thumb against the pads of my fingers, not wanting to learn more. I shook my head, but my hands were moving on their own, shifting the report of Dorothy Wise to the side.

The following report contained a colorful picture of a young woman covered in bruises. One eye was swollen shut, and her lip was busted open, but I could see she was beautiful. Long blonde hair and the one eye that remained open was a deep blue, but the pain and desperation captured in that photo turned my stomach.

I moved the picture aside to see the police report was from our local department. I winced when I saw the name.

Nik spoke for me. "Angela Wise. Rob's third wife. She filed for divorce in April of last year."

The police report was from May.

"What happened?" I asked.

"The divorce paperwork was withdrawn," Nik answered. "But... Keep—

"No," I said, pushing the papers away and standing. I glared at Nik, who was less than a foot away from me and staring down into my eyes. "I've read enough. Just tell me how this happens. How did he get away with it?"

Nik's eyes began to thaw as I stared up at him. A stillness settled into my apartment as neither of us moved for a long moment. My question filled with rage and despair began fading as Nik's presence swam through me.

"Sofia," he whispered my name, caressing it as he breathed, and my skin tingled. Warmed. Anticipated. My eyes lingered on his full, beautiful lips, but he sighed and turned away. "Angela was pregnant when she filed the police report."

"Was..."

"She lost the baby," Nik filled in what I didn't want him to say. "But she's pregnant again."

I closed my eyes, trying to process how I felt about that. Poor Angela was pregnant with a monster's baby.

Then Nik turned his shoulder toward me, and I opened my eyes to see his dark, onyx eyes once again peering down at me. His lips slowly curled into a sly smile. "Rumor is, it's not his."

Stay

I stared dumbfounded at Nik, my mind still processing the implications of what he'd told me.

"Before they got married, Angela owned her own Spa and Resort. A small start-up, but she was doing well enough for herself. Successful. Then she met Rob," Nik spoke as he moved back to the balcony, standing just inside the open door.

"How do you know all this?" I asked, stepping close behind him, as if I could reach out and grab him to stop him from leaving.

Nik shrugged with one of his broad shoulders. "That same friend I went to meet with. He's got a lot of resources that he shared with me."

"Is it all... legal?" I wasn't sure how much detail I wanted on that.

Nik chuckled; a deep smooth sound that pulled me even closer to him. "I can't vouch for him, but everything I've done is at least morally gray or above."

My eyebrows furrowed, and I crossed my arms, wanting a better explanation. Another chuckle answered me, richer and deeper this time, and my toes curled. His laugh was intoxicating.

"I talked to Angela."

"Oh." I blinked in surprise. That was something I hadn't expected.

Nik's face turned somber as his gaze returned to the night. "She's scared. She didn't outright tell me the baby wasn't Rob's, but there were enough hints. Like the fact she's terrified of what he'll do if he finds out the truth."

"But," I started, still in disbelief that Rob was something worse than just my misogynistic boss. Something much worse. "How can he get away with all this?"

"Deep pockets and family in the PD," Nik answered flatly.

I dropped my head as defeat clamped down on me. How was I any different if all the women before me couldn't get the help they needed? The hopelessness of the situation quickly sank in.

"Poor Angela," I muttered.

"He won't hurt her." Nik's voice had changed. Hardened. My eyes lifted to his face to find he was staring at me again. "Or you. I'm not going to let that happen."

Before I could process his cryptic words, he turned and took a step onto the balcony. I panicked, not wanting him to leave, and I followed before I could think about what I was doing. One hand reached out for his arm, and my fingertips barely brushed him when he spun, turning toward me and grabbing me by the hips. His grip on me was firm. Strong. The breath caught in my throat as our eyes locked for the briefest of moments before he looked down.

"Careful," he whispered.

I followed his gaze, and my eyes landed on the scattered glass I had forgotten about. Again. I had missed stepping on a shard by centimeters.

But I didn't care about the glass anymore. I didn't care about Rob Wise or all the terrible things he had done. The only thing I cared about were the hands still resting around my waist.

I reached out to grip his forearms, feeling the tense, strong muscles there, and I stared into his eyes. Dark onyx that threated to swallow me. Had his eyes always been so dark or was it the night?

I sucked my bottom lip into my mouth, teasing it between my teeth before I found the courage to plead, "Don't go."

"Sofia." The way he said my name, a pained and desperate whisper, had my body flushing from head to toe.

I took a single step backward into my apartment and tugged on his arms, pulling him with me. He followed. "Stay."

"I..." He licked his lips, and my eyes stayed glued to the movement, drinking in every little flick and twitch he made. "I'm afraid I won't be able to control myself."

My chest rose and fell with every deep breath, evidence of the fire growing within me. It pushed me forward, literally, and I pressed my body against his. My words were rough when I spoke. "We don't need control tonight."

My arms slipped around his neck, feeling every firm muscle on the way there, and his hands reacted, pulling me tighter against him. I softly moaned, tilting back to pull his head down to me. My mouth felt dry and parched, and I desperately needed him to fill my thirst.

An arm wrapped around my back, a hand caressing my bare skin and neck until his fingers tangled in my hair. Nik's body stiffened, and his hand fisted, gripping my hair so I couldn't move as his face hovered above mine. I whimpered against the building desires inside me that needed him to close that gap.

"I don't want to hurt you." His breath washed over me, and confusion mixed with the raw, lusty emotions swirling inside me. I couldn't concentrate.

"Hurt me?" It made no sense, but it was enough to stop my advance, even if the warmth in my body was still begging for more.

Nik dropped his forehead to mine, resting there as I tried to reign in my desires. Then, slowly, he lifted his head, brushing his nose against my cheek to reignite the fire within, but then he released me and stepped away. This time, he stepped further into my apartment instead of to the balcony.

I felt cold where he no longer touched me, and the night wind picked up, chilling me even further. I shivered and reached out to close the balcony door as if that would stop Nik from getting away. As soon as I locked the door, I turned to him and asked again. "How could you hurt me?"

A faint smile was on his lips, but it wasn't reflected in his eyes. "That friend, Greg, made me an offer to help solve the Rob problem. I took it. He's my employer now."

"You're not going back to the Press?" I gasped, feeling as if he was slipping further away.

"Not any time soon," he said. "But I can take care of Rob, so you don't have to worry about him anymore. The only thing..."

Nik trailed off, and I wrapped my arms around myself to ward away another chill. "What? How can you take care of Rob when the police can't?"

"Won't," he corrected. "They *won't* take care of him. So, Greg gave me something that would."

His words were cold and ominous. I let the silence linger until I couldn't take it anymore. "What did he give you?"

Nik's eyes dropped to the floor for a moment, but then he reached into his pocket and pulled out a small tube no bigger than my pinkie. He held it up, pinched between his thumb and index finger so that it caught the light. A dark liquid swirled inside, glittering through a spectrum of colors that danced on the surface.

It mesmerized me. Called to me.

Warning bells went off in the back of my mind, but I ignored them. Pushed them away. The only thing that mattered now was the black serum in the vial and the life that it promised.

DRINK

With a flick of his wrist, Nik turned his hand and palmed the vial, closing his fingers around it. As soon as it was out of sight, I blinked, suddenly aware that the small object had stolen all my focus.

Now, the fluorescent lights in the kitchen buzzed.

The refrigerator hummed.

The ceiling fan whirred.

All that had faded to nothing when my eyes were on the vial.

"What was that?" I gasped.

Nik glanced down at his closed fist before answering. "A choice."

I huffed at his answer, crossing my arms tightly and frowning. "I hope you have more of an explanation coming."

Those dark eyes fixed on me again, and one eyebrow rose as he took in my stance. A slight smirk tugged at the corners of his mouth, melting away my budding irritation. I had to admit his smile was cute, but the way he looked at me was damn sexy. I dropped my eyes as my skin flushed, unsure what to do next. I still wanted an explanation, but our attraction constantly muddled my thoughts. The alcohol wasn't helping either.

"I wish I could tell you everything, but…" he started, shifted as he reached out to run a finger down my bare arm. I sucked in a breath as he lit a fire along my skin from my shoulder to my elbow. "But Greg told me to keep it quiet."

As he pulled his touch away, I struggled to find the sensible woman in my head, begging her to retake control. I murmured one word that held no conviction. "Convenient."

He chuckled. "Isn't it?" He paused for a second before saying, "Look at me, Sofia."

I obeyed immediately, although I was surprised at how eagerly I had done so. I knew I should stand my ground on this, but that ground was falling away beneath me. Then his hand reached out to gently cup my chin, and I was lost.

"Even though I can't tell you everything, at least not right now, I promise I'll never lie to you."

And there he was, the sincere, honest, down-to-Earth Nik I had fallen for two weeks ago. I nodded before I had the chance to think it through. "Just tell me what you can."

"Greg gave me a way to take care of Rob. Legally." Nik dropped his hand and straightened before he added. "Or not so legally, if that's what you want."

My eyes widened in shock, and I was scared to ask what he was implying. Was he talking about blackmail? Threats?

Murder?

I swallowed and chose to ignore his last statement, at least for the moment. Instead, I reached out to lay a finger on his hand that held the vial. "Is this the way?"

"Part of it," he answered, raising his hand between us. "That's step one."

"Drugs?"

"No," he said. "It's more of an immunity. A failsafe if things go wrong."

My eyebrows furrowed as I peered into his eyes. "It's supposed to save you?"

"Not me," he said. "You."

"Me?" The word came out louder than I intended, but it didn't make sense. "I don't understand."

"I brought it for you." His voice dropped to a whisper. "In case I couldn't leave you tonight."

Before I could ask anything else, he opened his hand, and I was staring at the black liquid that quelled all my thoughts. There was no Rob. No mysterious Greg. No nefarious plans. It was just Nik and me and the vial between us.

My hand moved of its own accord, and I plucked the small cylinder from Nik's palm. Raising it high to catch the kitchen light, I tilted the vial back and forth, watching the liquid coat the glass. Red, blue, and green danced along the edges of the thick black serum. It was enchanting.

"You want me to drink it?"

"Yes, but," Nik answered. "It could change you if..."

His words trailed away, and my eyes flicked to him for a second, but they couldn't stay off the serum for long. "If what?"

"If I can't control myself."

I finally brought my hand down, wrapping my fingers around the vial and holding it close to my chest. I wasn't willing to give it back now that I had it. "Is losing control such a bad thing?"

"Not if you drink that."

"And you want me to drink it?"

Nik didn't answer right away. Instead, he stared at me long and hard as I stared back, refusing to back down. Finally, he replied, "Yes, but it's selfish of me when you don't know the consequences yet. Greg might—"

My thumbnail dug in and popped the cork from the top of the vial. Nik went silent as his eyes dropped to my hand. I only had one question left. "And this will help me *take care* of Rob?"

Nik's gaze rose to mine, and a smile slowly spread across his face. The way he looked at me was both wicked and delicious. "Yes."

Fuck it.

I raised the vial to my lips and let my tongue flick across the rim. Nik's eyes were drawn to my mouth, watching my every movement. Bitterness dried my tongue as I tested the liquid, followed by the briefest hint of sweetness that promised something more. Then, without another thought, I upended the vial and gulped it down.

The serum burned as it slid down my throat, thick and heady. It warmed me from within, spreading from my chest to my belly and riding my veins to the tips of my fingers and toes. It invaded my entire being with an intoxication that put the earlier alcohol to shame.

I reached up to pull my hair away from the heat of my face and shoulders and opened my eyes to see Nik staring. His eyes were half-lidded and glued to me, roving my body with each movement I made. Never in my life had a man looked at me that way. Finally, I couldn't stand it any longer.

My lips parted as I breathed, and I waited until Nik's eyes found my own. "We don't need control tonight."

And I turned toward my bedroom without a doubt that he was following behind.

The Fire Inside

I thought I was sexy. I thought I was seductive. I thought there was no way Nik could resist me, and then the room began to spin. As I swayed, I paused, doing my best not to stumble but failed. I changed direction, aiming for the couch because I knew I wasn't making it to my bed. The dizziness grew with each step I took until it threatened to overtake me, and everything went sideways.

I never hit the floor.

Instead, I hung weightless, floating in the middle of my living room and not understanding how. I opened my eyes but only caught glimpses of the space around me before the spinning forced me to close them again. In the brief glimpses I got, Nik was hovering over me, strong and protective, and I knew he had caught me.

I was in his arms, and I couldn't even feel it.

Dammit!

"Sofia." My name was whispered against my cheek, and I struggled to open my eyes again. I found myself on the couch, stable and still, but the dizziness refused to let go. "Sofia?"

I could only answer with a muffled groan. My tongue felt swollen and dry in my mouth. I thanked the stars I wasn't nauseated, at least not yet. If the vertigo didn't calm down soon, I surely would be.

"It should pass soon," Nik whispered over me, his words echoing in my head. "It hit me hard too. Maybe not this hard, but still."

As he spoke, the dizziness began to abate as long as I didn't move my head. I opened one eye and found I could focus if I squinted. I could see the concern on Nik's face as he guarded over me, and I smiled at the comfort that it brought.

"Uhm," I tried to speak, but my tongue was still too swollen and clumsy. I swallowed, working moisture back into my mouth, and tried again. "Okay?"

That was the only word I managed to get out, and I wasn't entirely sure it was comprehensible. Through my one squinting eye, I watched Nik smile down at me. "Yes, You're okay."

I took a deep breath and closed my eyes, relaxing into the fresh sensations the vial had given me for several minutes. Gentle waves of numbness and calm undulated through my body as I sank deeper into the couch. It almost felt like the cushions could swallow me whole, and it would feel fantastic while I was being absorbed into my living room furniture.

I giggled.

Then a realization hit me, and my eyes popped open. "I'm high!"

The words rang clear and true, causing Nik to chuckle softly beside me. "I guess you are. You'll come down quickly, I think. The peak doesn't last long."

"I feel all warm and fuzzy inside," I murmured, writhing on the couch as I let all my worry, pain, and anger go. "I've never felt so good."

A finger traced down my arm, all the way from my shoulder to my wrist. My attention was back on Nik, watching his face as he drank in my movements. Then his eyes locked back onto mine, and he said, "I'm going to make you feel even better."

A thrill went through me, and I sucked in a breath as his head lowered to my arm. He breathed soft kisses over my shoulder and steadily moved up until he nuzzled against my neck, sending goose-flesh rippling along my bare skin. His lips teased the tip of my earlobe, and I giggled as I shivered.

"That tickles," I murmured, but I didn't pull away. I was afraid if I did, he would stop. That was the last thing I wanted to happen.

"How do you feel now?" he whispered against my ear, his breath washing over me and causing me to squirm.

I twisted on the couch, sitting up so I could reach him, touch him. My hand went to his neck so my fingers could finally run through his dark, silky hair. The thick strands slid between my fingers and brushed against my palm. He stared down at me, his eyes drinking me in. My toes curled as I leaned toward him until my lips touched his cheek. I trailed kisses down his jawline and over his collarbone, feeling him tense beneath my lips.

"Sofia," he whispered, pulling me closer, and I gave in to the urge to wrap my arms around him, tugging him to me. His lips were firm and demanding as they devoured mine. I relented, wanting, *needing* him to devour me. His kiss was bruising. His body tight against my own. I clawed at his shirt, tearing away fabric and exposing flesh. My hands roamed over his firm chest with a rising, desperate need.

Nik's mouth left mine and traveled down my neck, kissing and licking every inch of exposed skin. His teeth nipped at my throat, causing me to cry out. A low grunt escaped him when my fingers dug into his back, urging him to continue.

"Sofia," his whisper came again, this time more urgent and strained. I rose high enough from the couch to slip one leg around him until he was between my thighs. My skirt, an afterthought and a nuisance, slid up to my waist, exposing nearly everything except the most intimate part of me that the lace of my panties still protected. I wrapped my legs tight around him and pulled our bodies together until I could feel all of him against me.

Nik froze, his gaze full of wild desire as he stared down at me, scorching me. His hands went to my hips and held me still, and I obeyed, ceasing my soft wriggling, but I couldn't hold back fully.

"What do you want?" I whispered, needing to hear him say it, needing to hear his thoughts.

He bent forward and kissed me once more, hard and fast, before he answered, "You, Sofia. Only you."

"Then take me," I pleaded, arching into him as I buried my hands in his hair and pulled him to me. Our mouths clashed together, and I sucked in air as I lost myself in him. All sense of reality vanished as I spiraled into a place where only lust existed.

Fabric tore and was ripped away, then I felt him. Warm and hard and demanding. I moaned into his mouth, and his fingers dug into my hips as he pushed deep into me. There was no hesitation or awkwardness, just a fierce need to be joined that consumed us both. I threw my head back and cried out, my voice strained as he filled me, stretching me beyond my limits. I clung to him, forcing my body to accept his, wanting to become one with him.

In my frenzy, I wasn't even aware Nik was losing control. Nor did it even register what was happening as his teeth sunk into my neck. Fire raced through my veins from the inside out, and I was drawn under by a wicked, beautiful frenzy.

Awake

I shifted, feeling the weight of a body against me, holding me, caressing me. My eyes fluttered open, and I found Nik staring at me in concern. It stole my breath. I didn't even remember falling asleep. I lifted my head off the pillow and tried to sit up, but ended up wincing in pain and sucked in a breath as I rolled my head from side to side. Glancing around, I realized I was in my bedroom.

"What happened?" The words came out choked, and I cleared my throat. My neck felt stiff. "What time is it?"

My fingers searched the covers and found my chemise was gone. I looked down and saw the evidence of that fact peeking out from under the sheets. I shyly pulled the covers over me, but the memories filled my head, full of ecstasy and pain. I remembered screaming out at one point, maybe two, but was it in pleasure or terror? That part was hazy.

Nik gently reached out to stroke my hair, and I watched him warily, my mind still foggy from whatever had happened between us. "Early morning. Not close to dawn yet. How are you feeling?"

"Groggy," I muttered, closing my eyes.

"That should pass soon," he said. "Sofia..."

His voice trailed off in a manner that demanded my attention. I focused on his face, searching for what he needed to tell me. A flash of fear shot through me when I saw the concern in his expression. "Nik?"

Nik buried his head against me, and I accepted the contact. Something raw and exposed about the gesture had me reaching my arms out to wrap around him. Finally, the tension seemed to release from him, and he cuddled tighter against me, using my head as a resting spot for his cheek. His whisper was hot on my skin. "I'm sorry. I lost control."

The memories swirled inside me, and I knew with certainty the blame didn't lay solely on him. I had been the one clinging to him, pulling him to me, desperate to have him inside me. A haunting sensation nagged at me, though, hinting there was more to it than that. I softly brushed my fingers against his stubbled cheek and asked, "Why is that a bad thing?"

"Because," he said softly, stroking my hair. "I changed you."

That gave me pause. My question came out uncertain. "Is that a bad thing?"

He hesitated before answering, "If you didn't want to be changed, then yes, it's bad. There's no going back."

I stared at him for a while longer before I said, "So... if it's too late, what now?"

Nik lifted his head to meet my eyes. "You'll be hungry soon if you're not already."

"I am," I admitted, but I wasn't surprised to feel the twinge of hunger. It had been hours since I ate the wings at the bar.

He studied me for a moment before he said, "We might need to talk about this later. If you're already feeling it, it will only get worse fast." His lips twitched up in a small smile. "Luckily, I know the perfect place to grab a bite."

Nik rose, sliding out from underneath me like I was nothing. He cast a look back at me as I sat in the bed and gave me a wink. He quickly collected his clothes before turning to disappear from my bedroom. I jumped up in my haste to follow, somehow finding my skirt was still wrapped around my waist. I smoothed it down over my hips and staggered after him.

"Why the rush?" I called out.

"You'll feel it soon," he answered, stepping back into view and tossing something toward me. "We have to hurry."

I snatched the object from the air and was surprised to find it was a wad of fabric. A second later, I realized it was the shirt I had worn to work the day before. With a smirk, I slid it on, knowing how much flesh it would expose without the chemise underneath. I stepped into the light and noted Nik's approving glance.

He glided forward and swept me into his arms for a long, passionate kiss that I didn't expect. Instantly, I was driven wild with need, wanting him again. I wanted to feel his hardness inside me, taste his blood on my tongue, and hear him scream my name, but he pulled away, leaving me breathless.

My hands went to my head as the rush of raw emotions crashed through me and faded just as quickly as they came. I was dizzy with it, and Nik reached out to steady me with a hand on my shoulder, but that was the only contact between our bodies.

"I'm sorry," he said, but he was hiding a smirk. "That's part of the change. We'll explore that later after you've had something to eat."

Before I could ask, he said, "Come on," and tossed me my heels.

At this point, it seemed easier to just obey him. Besides, the hunger he had warned me about was already growing. I bent to slip on my shoes but noticed the bandage was missing from my wound. I hunched over, poking at the sole of my foot, and was surprised it wasn't there. My eyes shot to the balcony, where the floor was still littered with glass.

Nik met my confused stare and simply said, "Change."

He held his hand to me, and I took it, allowing him to lead me from my apartment. I kept silent as we walked, not sure what to say. I had gone into that night unsure of my feelings for Nik, but now, I knew he was my everything. I was ready for him to consume me. Whatever this change was, it felt natural, and I was prepared to embrace everything that came with it.

My belly rumbled with hunger, and my tongue flicked over a sharp canine, sharper than I remembered it being. Nik squeezed my hand as he smiled down at me, and all my confusion fled. I returned a wicked smile.

Yes, change was good. This change was right.

Midnight Walk

T he breeze caressed my bare skin as I stepped out onto my landing. It lacked warmth, but the chill present earlier in the night was now missing. We were well past midnight, but I knew that dawn was still over an hour away. The change was working within me.

Nik closed my door, and I didn't even bother to lock it. Instead, I turned to Nik when he paused and looked up at him quizzically. "How do you feel?"

A sly smile ran across my face. "Hungry."

Starving, in fact, but I tried to ignore it. It seemed wrong to be excited about something so mundane, but the urge was almost... violent.

"Come," he whispered and led me down the steps. I followed more slowly, my gaze turning out into the night. The moon had set hours ago, and the sky was clear enough that stars were visible. Few people were out at this hour. It was that calm hour after all the drunks had fallen asleep and the working world had yet to wake. The world was filled with serene silence, and it belonged to me. No one could see what I was becoming, and no one could stop it.

I reached the ground floor, still following the shadow in front of me, but I could clearly make out Nik's broad shoulders. A thrill went through me, but it took me a few steps to realize that it wasn't caused by Nik. Not this time, at least.

I stopped, my gaze turning to the first-floor apartment and the open window.

Vince and Joe's apartment.

My mouth was dry, and I licked my lips, trying to wet them as I stepped forward, reaching out to the window frame.

"No," Nik said, grabbing my wrist. His touch burned through me, and my first instinct was to jerk away, but he continued. "They're your friends."

"But," I muttered and closed my eyes as the aroma from their apartment drifted to me.

The tug on my wrist was insistent and demanding. Finally, I reluctantly pulled away from the tempting scent to peer up at Nik. "Trust me."

"What are they cooking in there at this hour?" I asked in my confusion. "It smells so good."

"Come," he whispered again, and this time I allowed him to pull me away. Then, casting one last look over my shoulder, I faced forward and refused to look back. There was a strange energy in the air, a feeling of anticipation that made my stomach clench.

We walked. First, it was out of my apartment parking lot, then deep into suburbia. We passed several houses, and I had an itching sensation alerting me to the presence of people inside.

But we slipped through the neighborhood unseen. Two shadows drifting silently adjacent to normalcy. The further we went, the surer I became that a life such as that was behind me now.

Mile after mile, we walked through the city until we eventually turned down a street that was quiet and dark. Nik hadn't spoken for over thirty minutes, but I knew where we were going. This road led to the lonely and deserted side of the Morning Press. At this early hour, there would only be a handful of people there.

Rob would be one of them.

The man had a habit of working late and arriving early, or at least he made sure people believed he did. I knew he was no over-achiever. It was simple posturing for appearance. The only thing upper management cared about.

I scoffed.

"Did I mention?" Nik's voice whispered low beside me. "What happened to Rob's second wife?"

My breath hitched, and I stuttered, "I don't believe you did?"

He stopped before the large building and murmured, "She disappeared just a year after they were married."

"Wha—" I cut myself off abruptly, the words dying on my lips as I stared up at the building. My belly rumbled with hunger and anger. I felt Nik's eyes weighing me, watching for my reaction. It came as a single step forward.

"Wait," he said. "Do you understand why we're here?"

I froze and stared at him. His hand tightened on mine, and I looked into his eyes. They were cold and calculating, and my confusion melted away. My voice was rough as I said, "He won't hurt Angela."

Nik nodded his approval and asked, "You want to go up alone?"

"No," I replied as I forced my feet forward. "Come with me."

There was no more hesitation. We moved together to the doors.

REVENGE

We slipped into the building easily enough, the silence thick and oppressive around us. The overhead lights were off or dimmed, creating eerie shadows in every corner, and adrenaline trickled through my veins, mixing with the insatiable hunger. We didn't exactly sneak, but no one noticed our passing. If the security guard saw us on his cam feed, he raised no alarms.

We ghosted through the halls of the lower floor, and as we stepped into the elevator, Nik broke the silence. "Are you ready?"

"Yes," I answered quickly, confidently. What came out was nearly a snarl. Nik's nod was grim, and the silence returned as the elevator went up, dinging at each floor as we passed.

One...

Two...

Three...

Four...

The doors opened, and the reassuring grip Nik had on my hand released, and I glanced back at him, flexing my empty fingers.

"I'll be right behind you," he whispered.

I watched him for a while, staring into his eyes, missing the courage his touch provided, but then my stomach rumbled with hunger. He nodded in silent reassurance, and I turned back to the rows upon rows of empty desks that stretched into the void.

I became a shadow, prowling through the cubicles as the darkness wrapped around me. The main overhead lights were dark, leaving the solitary beam that trickled from under Rob's door the only illumination. The hunger gnawed at me relentlessly, urging me to move forward. It didn't let me consider my actions or the consequences. All it cared about was the beating heart and the warm lifeblood flowing in the veins of Robert Wise. My silent footfalls guided me through the cubicle labyrinth straight for the light, drawn to it like a moth to a flame.

I paused just outside his doorway, breathing deep as I listened intently, straining to hear any sound beyond his door. I rhythmic *thump, thump, thump* was my reward, but it didn't sound like typing. Pressing my ear against the door, I could have sworn I heard panting. A low groan.

Then a woman's soft cries mewled from what seemed like a place very far away.

My lip curled in a snarl as my body responded, turning the knob before I could stop myself, but the door opened without a sound. The room beyond was bathed in the glow of a single desk lamp and the computer monitor Rob sat behind. He was engrossed in the screen, completely oblivious to my presence. The room smelled of stale coffee and sex, and it briefly overshadowed the mouthwatering aroma that had drawn me in.

I hovered in the shadows and watched. My eyes took in the sweat on his brow, the twisted smirk on his face, and the frantic thumping of his masturbation. He wore the company headset, but I could still hear the sounds of the porn he watched through the cheap earpiece.

My stomach roiled with anger and fury as the female screamed to stop. Her begging made it to my ears, and I thought of Rebecca Tyler and the unwanted contact in the kitchenette. Of Jessica Atwell, who was detained in the parking lot. Of Dorothy Wise, last seen in Arkansas over a decade ago.

And of Angela Wise, pregnant, terrified, and trapped with this monster.

The rage in my belly wound its way to my throat, burning with an insatiable thirst. The disgust for his wickedness morphed into a fierce hatred that intertwined with the need for vengeance. The barrage of emotions and need overwhelmed me, clouding my judgement and awakening something primal within.

I growled.

Rob flinched, violently, comically, rolling back in his chair and trying to rise to his feet, but his head jerked down, caught by the headset wire. All the while, he was trying to shove his junk back into his pants with one hand and shut down the video that was playing on his computer with the other.

"Who…" he coughed and sputtered, squinting into the shadows. So I took a step forward. "Sofia?"

With a final step, I stood before him, my teeth clenched as I held my breath, struggling to hold the rage and hunger within me in check.

"Sofia?" He stuttered my name again, finally righting himself as he yanked his headset off. "You… You got here early today."

My teeth ground tight as I held my response.

In the silence, Rob managed to find a false swagger after he adjusted his pants. "Finally going to get some work finished on time?"

The comment was on par for him, but it lacked his usual bite. The deep flush consuming his neck told the true story. I could smell his nervousness, itching the tip of my nose, edging out the scent of his coffee. It was enough for me to relax my jaw, and the hint of a grin pulled at my lips.

Rob stared at me, and when I didn't speak, he grew even more flustered. His eyes twitched, glancing down at my hands, my hips, my breasts. Twice they flicked back to my eyes, then back to my breasts before he formulated his next thought.

"Wasn't that the shirt you wore yesterday?" He ogled, staring at my chest and the curve of my waist, as if his question gave him excuse enough. I threw my shoulders back, giving my breasts a small bounce, and his eyes widened with desire, and that awful, smirk twisted his lips again. Lust swirled in his eyes, and the bulge in his pants rose again.

My stomach rumbled, and my throat burned.

I shifted, and a few quick steps took me behind his desk. My own speed shocked me as I found myself staring up at him.

"Sofia?" He was back to unsure, but didn't look bothered by my invasion of his space.

Well, that would change soon.

With one hand on his shoulder, I slammed his body back into the chair. He rocked back with enough force to tip himself backward, but I caught the arm of the chair and pulled him to face me.

"What the hell?" he gasped, and I leaned over him to reply.

I sneered, "You disgust me."

The uncertainty that broke over him was so satisfying, I had to focus on keeping my face blank as I savored it. Behind his heated skin and generic aftershave, I could smell him and the fear that tinged the edges of his scent, a tantalizing aroma that teased the predator that was waking inside me.

"I see what's happening here," he started, although it was a clear attempt to regain control of the situation. "You want to earn a favor so I'll give you a pass on those articles, don't you? You wouldn't be the…"

CRACK.

The sound of my hand slapping the side of his face resonated through the room. The grin finally bloomed on my face, sadistic and terrible, as I considered the pain I'd inflicted. It was nothing compared to what he had done to those women.

Rob's head lolled back, then to the side before sliding forward until his chin rested on his chest. He groaned, not exactly having lost conciousness, but definitely dazed.

"You bitch," he muttered, a hand going to his cheek as he tested his jaw.

"Aw," I cooed, reaching out to pluck at a few strands of his gelled hair that now stuck up in wild and wayward angles. "I think I messed up your hair."

His hand came up to grab my wrist, his movement slowed by the daze. His grip, however, was strong and tight. Rob raised his eyes to mine, and the haze in them cleared to reveal his anger. "What the fuck do you think you're doing?"

A surge of satisfaction rippled through me as his grip tightened on my wrist. I leaned over him as he shied back, and my voice dripped with venom as I whispered, "What am I doing? Isn't it obvious, Mr. Wise? I'm here to make you pay."

Rob's eyes widened, a flicker of fear crossing his face as he realized the severity of his situation. His grip loosened slightly, but I could still feel his fingers digging into my skin. I watched as the confidence drained from his expression, replaced by confusion.

"Pay?" he stammered. Did I hear the tiniest little quiver in his voice? "You're delusional. I think it's time for you to go."

"Rebecca Tyler." I said the name simply, and I waited for his reaction, curious what he would do.

"Who?"

I cocked my head to the side, taking note that his confusion seemed genuine. I tried again. "Jessica Atwell."

There. A flicker of recognition lit his eyes. His hand that was still on my wrist jerked me forward. "Whores. Both of them," he hissed in my face. "They enjoyed it."

"Where's Dorothy?" I said easily, almost gently, despite his aggression.

Rob's eyes widened, and his grip on my wrist tightened once again. The smell of fear grew thicker, but anger masked his face. He stood, trying to push me back in the process, but he stumbled when I didn't allow him to move me. His jaw flexed for a moment as he considered, then he stepped against me and growled, "It's your word against mine. I'll have you out on your ass before the first bell."

"No," I answered, letting a grin twist my lips. "I don't think you will."

Justice

Rob sneered. He was in unfamiliar territory, and his face contorted as he tried to process the unexpected turn of events. His confidence was on unknown and shaky ground, and my tongue slid across the edge of my teeth as I waited, biding my time, savoring everything about it.

His fists clenched at his sides, teeth grinding and nostrils flaring. I couldn't decide if his display was an attempt to frighten me, or his frustration showing as his control slipped away. It didn't matter, but it was fun to watch. At least for a bit. The hunger demanded I end my games.

My voice was hushed, barely above a whisper. "What did you do to Dorothy?"

The tension thickened as the words hung in the air. For a moment, Rob hesitated, his expression shifting from anger to confusion to something else entirely. Then he lunged, hands grabbing for me that never made contact. I shifted and balled my fist, sharply jabbing him in the chest. The power of the blow surprised me, sending Rob flying backwards to land in his chair and roll until he crashed into the wall. He hit hard enough that it tipped over, spilling him onto the floor. His body twisted awkwardly before he rolled to his stomach.

"Fuck!" Rob's wheeze was further muffled by the carpet, and he gasped in a ragged breath. He tried to rise, but I stepped on his shoulder, driving him back to the floor. He struggled against the weight of my foot, but it was futile.

"What happened to her?" I asked again, my voice low and measured. There was no rush in my tone, only patience, and I watched the muscles beneath his skin jump as he struggled to breathe. I wasn't even using all my strength.

I released him so he could turn, looking up at me with shock plastered on his face. His expression twisted into an ugly grimace. "You bitch."

He scrambled up, but I stepped away, keeping my distance. He didn't advance. In fact, the heady aroma of fear clung to him, saccharine and enticing as it grew stronger. At least he was learning how little power he had over me.

Rob wiped at his face, smearing a thin line of red-tinged saliva. My eyes closed, and I bit my lip as I stifled a moan. I could smell the blood, and it wasn't enough. I needed more. I needed that smell to permeate the room.

"What happened?" I repeated.

"Sofia," he started, my name sounding like gravel grinding between rocks.

I arched an eyebrow, cocking my head to the side as I gave him my sweetest smile. "Yes, Rob?"

"Let's take a step back," he spat out, fumbling over the words as his hands patted the air in an attempt to calm the situation. "Let's talk about this like adults."

I laughed, his words catching me off guard. No begging, no barga ining... yet.

"Don't you dare laugh," Rob growled, but his voice sounded weak. His hand came out to point an accusing finger at me.

I folded my arms across my chest, motioning for him to go on. I didn't care what he had to say. I just wanted to watch him squirm a bit longer.

"The Holden research from last... last week," Rob started, but stumbled over his words as I raised an eyebrow. My gaze focused on his shaking fingers, and I welcomed the twisted grin that hadn't fully left my face. That only made his shaking worse. "I can fix the files. Turn it over to print under your name. You'll get the all the recognition for solid work."

My laughter spilled out then, and I slapped a hand over my mouth. "Are you fucking kidding me?" I managed through my giggles, sur-prised by how inflated his sense of self-worth was. "My presentations are better than yours."

My movement was swift, easy, as I reached out to touch the side of his face, then brutally slammed his head down onto the desk. He fell forward onto his knees, his eyes unseeing.

"You're not even good enough to clean my office," I snapped, and I leaned over him as I spoke. It would make no difference. Nothing could shatter Rob's infallible ego. "Now, tell me where Dorothy is."

The dazed man stared up at me, his face slack. His breathing was shallow, and his hands were limp at his side.

"I can help you," he croaked, voice hoarse.

"How?" I asked, reaching my thin arms around his chest and yank-ing him off the floor to toss him over his desk. My grip tightened around his throat, threatening to cut off his words and his access to oxygen. But I couldn't let go. I couldn't let him live. He didn't deserve a second chance. Not after what he had done.

"Please," he breathed, struggling against the daze as much as the pressure I used to hold him down. "I swear I can help you."

"Help," I breathed, leaning closer. "Isn't what I want from you."

His eyes widened, clarity seeping in past the daze as the realization dawned on him. I finally received what I had been waiting for. The room flooded with the scent of his terror, and I breathed it in, intoxicated by it.

Then another scent hit me. Cold. Coppery.

Delicious.

My throat burned as the deepest thirst I could ever imagine barreled into me.

Rob was scrambling, reaching for his desk phone. I tore it from his hands. The cord snapped as I flung it against the wall, broken and useless, and I barely registered doing it. I didn't care. The only thing that mattered was reaching the source of that exquisite scent.

I jerked Rob up and threw him onto his back, seeing the wound on his temple where I had slammed his head against the desk. Bright red blood pulsed there, a thin line running down into his hair.

It called to me.

It sang to me.

Rob's struggles were growing stronger, frantic. His flailing only made me press down harder, and my nails dug into his flesh as I held him. His eyes were wide, pleading, and I knew he was fighting not to beg, because begging meant giving up. He sucked in air to yell, but my hand was there already, covering his mouth to stifle his screams. However, every thing I did, every movement, was all reactionary, instinctual.

It was the mesmerizing ruby-red liquid that captured my being. I crept closer, leaning forward as it drew in me. I had to have it.

Rob stilled. His eyes stared up at me, a mix of fear and panic swirling in the icy blue. A foreign expression, but delicious and satisfying to see. I sucked in a breath as the hunger overwhelmed me, and I felt my canines pulse, stretch, elongate. Fangs. The tools of my new life.

I leaned closer, my lips brushing against his temple, and my tongue darted out to taste the blood. A surge of ecstasy surged through my body as the warm, metallic taste flooded my senses. It was like liquid fire, the elixir of life that would satiate my being. My teeth sank into his flesh of his neck, piercing through the skin and into the pulsing vein beneath. Rob let out a muffled scream, but my hand pressed harder over his mouth, crushing his lips against his teeth. His body convulsing beneath me, but I paid no heed to his pain. All that mattered was the sweet nectar flowing into my mouth, nourishing me, fueling me.

As I drank, a surge of power coursed through my veins. Memories and emotions flooded my mind, fragments of Rob's twisted life, his victims, and the pain he had inflicted upon others. It was overwhelming, but it fueled my rage. The hunger transformed into a thirst for justice, a need to rid the world of monsters like him.

My grip on him tightened until the sound of bones cracked as his metallic life force ebbed into my mouth, down my throat. My hunger mixed with a perverse satisfaction. I drank as the visions blurred into satiation and the struggles of the man beneath me grew weaker and weaker. When nothing remained except exhaustion and deathly coldness, I slowly pulled away, releasing Rob Wise as his blood dripped down my chin. Glassy and vacant eyes stared up at the ceiling, unseeing. The sound of my labored breathing broke the eerie silence.

I took a step back, wiping the blood from my lips with my fingers, a mix of satisfaction and sadness washing over me. The taste of vengeance was bittersweet. The hunger had been tamed for now, but the darkness within me had been stirred. It was silent, waiting, but it would forever be there.

A surge of guilt washed over me, but it was quickly replaced by a sense of liberation. Rob was a monster, a predator that had haunted the lives of the women around him. In that moment, I felt like an avenging angel, delivering justice on behalf of the innocent.

There was no sound from behind me, but I knew he was there. I said softly, "I know where Dorothy is."

Nik emerged from the shadows, his eyes filled with a mix of understanding and concern. He reached out to touch my arm, his fingers gently tracing along my shoulder, grounding me in this newfound reality. "Dead?"

I nodded. In those moments I held Rob's life in my hands, he had shown me everything. Every terrible, dark deed he had committed on those poor women. "She wasn't the only one."

Nik took my hand. "And he isn't the only one."

I finally turned away from Rob's corpse and looked into Nik's eyes, the weight of what he was saying sinking in. He took my hand and squeezed, and I squeezed back, accepting what I had become. As we walked back through the silent halls, a sense of purpose filled me. I realized that this was just the beginning. There were many more like Rob out there, preying on the weak and vulnerable.

Together, Nik and I would become the hunters, seeking out those who deserved punishment and delivering it with ruthless precision. The night belonged to us now, our dark hunger fueling our every step.

As the first hint of dawn painted the sky, we sank below the city to the safety of the darkness. The cloak of shadows enveloping us. I fully embraced the change within me. The hunger, the violence, the power—they were the tools that made up who I was. Tools I would use to protect the innocent, to enact justice, and to ensure that no abuser would get away unscathed. The transformation had awakened a part of me that I had always known existed, but had never fully embraced. It was a part that thirsted for righteousness, for retribution, and for the thrill of the hunt.

The world would forever be full of monsters, but they would know that they could never hide from the shadows. For in the darkness, justice was waiting, ready to strike. And as long as I lived, I would be there, lurking in the shadows, ready to unleash the darkness within me.

About the Author

Debra Rose is the author of The Phoenix Curse series, a bestseller in Amazon's post-apocalyptic and dystopian science fiction genre. Although she previously published under the pen name D.R. Johnson, all her new and current novels will be published under her full name. Debra is currently pursuing her bachelor's in arts at Southern New Hampshire University, and she lives in Texas with her husband and two children.

Debra specializes in science fiction and the supernatural, although she has been known to stray into the realms of fantasy from time to time. Her books have graced the top of Amazon's bestseller lists and continue to captivate fans of the genre. Passionate about her craft, Debra loves to write enthralling stories that focus on character development during apocalyptic situations.

Also By

The Phoenix Curse

When the red mist came, it left few unchanged, most for the worst.

The Walk

It's the buzzing in my head that disturbs me the most. It comes as a warning, right before they do.
The little black spiders that are eating our world.